Joe's Most Dangerous Mission

Doris' Works

Thoughts Feelings Visions Memories
How to Survive on A Little
I'll Wait
Love Has No Color
Joe's Most Dangerous Mission
(Sequel to I'll Wait)

Future works

Who Did It?
A Miracle for Sarah
Adventures of Charlie

Joe's Most Dangerous Mission

Sequel to I'll Wait

Doris M. Jones

 www.trafford.com

North America & international
toll-free: 1 888 232 4444 (USA & Canada)
fax: 812 355 4082

CONTENTS

INTRODUCTION

Joe and Lydia Stevenson have been married five years now, and their story continues from I'll Wait. When they met, it was like a puzzle fitted together. They had so much in common with each other. Joe's best friend Steve had introduced them.

Joe was happy to be home. Even though it was four years since his discharge from the Army, he thanks God for letting him make it back to his family. All of his life he dreamed of having a family and being very much in love.

Now that he has found that, he doesn't want anything to change it. They have three children and are very happy. What Joe and Lydia don't know it that their lives are about to be turned upside down. Joe was the Leader of a Tactic Team who rescued captured Soldiers while he was in the Army.

When he got discharged, he held the best and highest record for a Tactic Team Leader for rescues. As you read the story, you will discover what happens and how they handle it. Will this end their marriage? An event that is about to take place might throw them off their feet. Will their love be strong enough to hold them together?

CHAPTER 1

JOE AND LYDIA ARE VERY HAPPY

It's been four years since Joe's last Secret Mission. They now have three children, Joseph 4, Linda 3 and Scott 2. Lydia has her hands full but loves every minute of taking care of her family. And Joe can't wait to get home every day from work to help with the children. He loves playing with them.

Lydia and Joe read and pray with their children before they go to bed at night. After they put them to bed, they have time to sit and talk about their day. Joe loves Lydia to update him on the children. He wants to know all the new things they do and say. He loves being a husband and father. All of his life he's dreamed of a family.

His greatest joy was when each of the children began walking and talking. They take a lot of pictures of the children on a regular basis. Joseph and Linda love looking at their pictures as well as Joe and Lydia.

They are blessed to have both sets of grandparents living near them. Sometimes the grandparents get together with the grandchildren and other times they take turns having them in their homes.

Joe and Lydia's parents alternate keeping the children on Fridays so that they can go on their weekly date. Usually, they keep them over-night. Of course, the children love spending the night with their grandparents.

Joe said to Lydia, "I am so thankful that our parents live near us because it would be hard to let a stranger babysit our children. I would be so afraid to let just anyone watch them."

"Well, Joe, we have God to thank for that. But I am as happy as you are about this. People are doing strange things to children these days," said Lydia.

Joe told Lydia when he was discharged from the Army, "We will have a date one night each week, and we will always be courting and in love. I want you to know that I will always love and appreciate you."

"I am with you on that. If we both want it, we can do it," Lydia said. "This will give the children a break from us too."

Joe was able to get a job paying $35.00 an hour. They saved for four years so they could buy their home. Lydia worked until Scott turned one year old. She had a good job also. And when they were single, they had nice savings.

They set their mortgage for fifteen years. Since they had put a big down payment, it wouldn't take them long to pay it off. Their home had four bedrooms, three baths, a family room and a large backyard. That was perfect for Joseph, Linda, and Scott.

When Joseph and Linda woke up, they ran into the kitchen. Lydia had Scott in a high chair. They gave Lydia, a kiss and said,

"Good morning Mommie," in unison. They also kissed Scott. They both laughed as usual because this happened a lot.

Lydia asked, "Where is Daddy? Did you all wash up and brush your teeth?"

They said, "Yes, Daddy helped us. He's getting the newspaper."

"Good," Lydia said. "Are you all ready to eat? Breakfast will be ready in about ten minutes, and you guys can fill your little tummies."

Joseph said, "I am ready to eat, Mommie."

Linda said, "Me too, Mommie."

Just then Joe came into the kitchen reading the paper. He looked up and said, "Looks like it's going to be a grand day to go to my favorite spot at the park."

He looked at Lydia and winked. She gave him a broad smile. Then he went over and kissed her.

"Good morning," he said.

She said, "Good morning. Are you alright? You didn't sleep well last night."

"I was dreaming that I was on a Mission," he said.

"What's a Mission Daddy?" Joseph asked.

Joe answered by saying, "It's when you are instructed to go and do something for someone."

"Oh," said Joseph.

"Alright let's eat, so we can finish and do our chores. Then we will go to Daddy's favorite spot in the park," said Lydia.

Joseph and Linda said, "Yeah, yeah, we are going to the park."

Joe said, "Honey when the children are older, we can have a swimming pool put in. What do you think?"

Lydia replies, "I think it's a fantastic idea. In the meantime, you can take the children to the park pool and teach them to swim. They will love it."

Joe called Joseph and Linda. They both came running. They said at the same time, "Yes Daddy?"

"Would you guys like to learn to swim?" Joe asked.

"Yes, Daddy." They always answered at the same time. They looked at each other and laughed.

Lydia said, "You can tell that you all are related." She turned and went into the living room.

"Give me a couple of weeks. I will take you all to the park pool and teach you how to swim," Joe said.

They ran to Lydia and told her, "Daddy is going to teach us how to swim."

"Did Daddy tell you all that we are getting a pool when you are older?" Lydia asked.

"Yes, and Daddy is going to teach us to swim," they replied again.

Joseph went into the backyard, looking as if the pool was already there. He was excited because they loved playing in the water. Joe thought this would be great for them in the summer, especially when it was hot. He usually connected a sprinkler to the water hose and sprayed the children when it was hot. In the meantime, back in the house, Joe looked at Lydia as she was wiping tears from her eyes.

He said, "Honey is something wrong?"

"Oh no, I am just happy," she said.

Joe walked over to her and pulled her close to him. They stood hugging for a moment; then he kissed her on her forehead.

He said, "I think when you were pregnant with Joseph and I didn't know, it would have been difficult for me. I could have been injured or killed, and you would have been by yourself."

Lydia said, "Joe, I have dreams about what I would have done if something would have happened to you. Each day I wake up, I thank God for bringing you back to me."

"I love you so much, Lydia. If I had known that you were pregnant, I would have had problems focusing on my job," he said.

"Well, I am thankful that I had my job and the baby to keep my mind occupied. It was so hard not knowing where you were or if you were safe," she said.

Joe said," I was upset that I couldn't tell you where I was going."

"It was especially hard not being able to write to you and get a response," Lydia said.

Joe told Lydia, "The day that we were at the park, I couldn't wait to hold you in my arms. I had dreamed of that day. Every chance I got, I took out your poem, "I'll Wait, and read it."

"Thank God, we are back together, and we can put that behind us," said Lydia.

Joe said, "Let's forget about that. I am back and living my dream. How long will breakfast be ready? I am hungry!"

"It will be ready in a few minutes. Get the children washed up and I will set the table. Do you want something to snack on while waiting?" She asked.

"No Baby, I think I can wait. I will get the crew washed up, and we will be patient," he said.

Joe called the children so they could wash up for breakfast. He had them to line up like soldiers at the bathroom door. That was a game he played with them, and they loved it. They would march like Soldiers. Joe enjoyed it as much as Joseph and Linda. They loved their parents so much.

They never played war games. Joe did not want to relive that part of his life. He was happy to be with his family and did not want anything to spoil it. He and Lydia played a lot of educational games with them.

When Joe brought the children in, he said, "If Mommie feels like it, maybe we can go to a movie after we leave the park."

"It sounds good to me. We haven't been to the movies in a while," replied Lydia. "Let's see which one Daddy picks."

"Daddy, what movie are we going to see?" Asked Joseph. "I like all of the Disney Movies about animals."

Joe responded, "It may be a Disney movie. We will have to check the list."

"I like Disney movies too," Linda said. As they finished eating.

Then Lydia said, "Alright everyone. Let's do our chores." Joseph and Linda went to their rooms. They made sure their toys were in the proper place. Joe went to the master bedroom while Lydia stayed and cleaned the kitchen. Joseph's job was emptying the kitchen trash, and Linda was responsible for the bathroom.

About thirty minutes later, Lydia said, "Is everyone ready to go?"

They scrambled to the door that leads to the garage and all said very quickly together,

"We are ready to go."

Joe had Scott in his arms as they headed for the car so that they can go to the park. Joe has always tried to take the children to see movies about every two months. He and Lydia have Friday nights each week for their date night. They are blessed to have their parents near them. Their parents alternate keeping the children for them. Joe and Lydia do not have siblings. Their children are the only grandchildren for their parents.

They finally arrived at the park. After they secured everything in Joe's favorite spot, he and the kids went off to play. Lydia decided to indulge in a book that she had wanted to read. After about two hours, Joe and the children came back to Lydia.

Joe said, "Honey, can you take over now? I feel a little tired. I think I'll take a nap."

"Are you alright?" Lydia asked.

He said, "I didn't sleep well last night. I am just a little tired."

Joe laid down, and Lydia took the children over to watch the ducks. The pond area was her favorite place. She loved watching the ducks chase each other. The kids liked the ducks too. They thought they were cute.

CHAPTER 2

JOE AND LYDIA MET

Joe remembered the first moment when he saw Lydia. He had waited for God to send him the right woman. His parents raised him to respect women. He learned that the Bible taught against sexual relationships before marriage.

As a teen, he decided that he was going to honor this because that's what the Bible teaches. He kept himself busy with sports, music and studying and he also was an honor student.

His best friend Steve had called and asked if he could come by his job for a few minutes. Joe agreed to meet Steve at his job. It was near the time for Steve to get off work. Joe hadn't seen him in about three weeks. He felt that Steve wanted to catch up on things with him.

It was a very hot day and he wanted some water. When he got there, he went inside. Just as he got in the door, Steve was passing near him. Steve told him to come with him, but when he reached his office, there was no Joe. Steve turned around, and Joe was not too far from the front door.

In the meantime, there was this beautiful young lady who lived about fifteen minutes from Joe, who had the same values as he did. Her name was Lydia. He remembered Steve had said he had something to show him. Joe had been to Steve's office many times. He never went in because he did not want to disturb the other employees. He had spotted this beautiful woman and his mouth was slightly open.

Steve smiled and went to him and grunted, "Would you like to meet her?"

Joe replied quickly, "Yes, indeed! If she is single."

Steve said, "Come on."

When they approached Lydia, she was focused on her work and didn't realize that they were by her desk. Right before Steve called her name, she looked up startled.

Steve said, "Lydia, I want you to meet my best friend, Joe."

When Lydia looked up, they locked eyes, smiling at each other and Steve was smiling at both of them. After the introduction, they were still smiling at each other.

Finally, Steve cleared his throat and said, "My friend, don't you have an errand to run?"

"I sure do," Joe answered, looking at Lydia and said, "May I call you?"

Joe thought, man you've never been this bold before. Don't put your foot in your mouth. You just met this woman.

"I-I guess so," was her reply."

Joe hurried on his way looking at Lydia and almost ran into the door. He thought meeting Lydia was the best thing that had happened to him. Before Joe met Lydia, he was beginning to wonder if he was going to meet the right woman. Joe was twenty-eight years old, and it finally happened.

He was nervous when he first asked Lydia for a date. On their first date, he took her to his favorite park. He prayed that she would love it. Joe felt if she liked the park, she was the lady for him. Lydia fell in love with the park. She told him that, "This is God's country." He knew then that she was the one.

It became their favorite place to hang out, and this is where they now take their children.

The first time he saw her in Steve's office, he got excited. He felt like a kid that had just gotten a new toy. When he picked her up for their first date, he told her that he was taking her to his favorite spot in the park. Lydia had teased him for calling it, "His spot."

That day he knew she was the lady for him. She fell in love with the park and the beauty of it. All Joe could think about after he took Lydia home was how beautiful she was and how she enjoyed the park.

Lydia was on the same page with Joe. She was sure that he was the right man for her.

Lydia remembered the guys she had dated just seemed to be looking for a bed partner. Sleeping around was something that she was not going to do.

When Lydia was a teen, she told her Mom that she was going to wait until she got married before having sex. So far, she had been able to abstain herself. She is now twenty-six years old and wondered if she was going to be an old maid. All of her friends had gotten married and often teased her.

They told her that a man wants to sample what he is getting. She told them the man that she marries would not have a problem because he will know that she wasn't sleeping around. She decided to stop dating and prayed that God would let her meet the right person.

Now she was sure that Joe was the man. He was very polite and a nice person. She thought he didn't try to kiss her good-night when he brought her home. She realized that he was different from the other guys.

That was a big plus in his favor because she had to fight off her previous dates. The more she and Joe dated, the more they realized that they had a lot in common. And they both felt that they were meant to be together.

This relationship was so different from any that either of them had ever had. They knew that they had met their mate. At one time, they were thinking the same thing, "I have found my love."

CHAPTER 3

THE TERRORIST GROUP

In the meantime, The Terrorist Group is getting their men and women in place. They have already taken inventory of their weapons and ammunition. They planned to have guards at the two entrances to the school. They had captured three hundred and fifty Villagers, and they were in the school. The area was very wooded, and the school was back from the street. All the grade levels are taught at this school because the community is small.

The Villagers were ordered to take sleeping bags and personal items with them. Colonel Von Swog figured it would be easy to keep track of everyone if they were in one place. The men and boys were on one side of the school and the women and girls on the other side.

Colonel Von Swog gave his group special instructions that no one was to be touched or hurt without his orders. It was sixty people in The Terrorist Group, and ten were women. They looked just as hard as the men in the group.

Since the Village only had about six hundred people, their school was only out for one month in the summer, and they kept it stocked with food. Also, they had a storage house on the grounds to make sure no one would go hungry if they were out of work.

The women in The Terrorist Group made plans for the Village women and girls to do the cooking and cleaning up afterward. It was a dark day in the Village. They had never experienced anything like this. They didn't have crime in their Village. Being held hostage was a very frightening time for them. The women were concerned about their husbands and sons. And the husbands were concerned about their wives and daughters. Colonel Von Swog met with his group briefly.

He said, "Our goal is to get the things that we have asked for and get out of here as soon as we can."

The Terrorist Group responded with, "Yes Sir."

Captain Schmidt said, "If they come at us and we get boxed in, what do we do?"

"We will only kill when necessary," said Colonel Von Swog. "I will divide you all into groups. Then you all will get instructions. We will meet at 1900 (7:00 p.m.) hour in the evening after we eat."

Enid Von Plat asked, "What if someone tries to escape?"

Colonel Von Swog said, "I don't think anyone is going to try to get away. All the windows have bars, and we have guards around the school."

The Village was isolated, and this was perfect for The Terrorist Group. The way the Village was it would be a task to get the hostages out safely. That's why the President wanted the best Tactic Team Leader to handle this.

Joe had never thought about the possibility of being called back to service. He and Lydia were sitting on the couch after putting their children to bed. The news came on with the event of a situation in Humi, Gerack in the country of Amerizon.

This little country is in the East that was barely on the map. It was about a vicious Terrorist Group. The newsman stated that they had taken over a Village of about six hundred people. It turned out that all the Villagers weren't hostages. Three hundred and fifty were hostages.

The Terrorist Group was organized and prepared for an attack. They had taken inventory of their weapons and ammunition, water and food. They set up guard posts so they could see in the distance.

Colonel Von Swog had the families separated. He knew that no one would try to escape not knowing where their other family members were. The Terrorists were ordered not to bother the women and girls by the Colonel. Since the Village was in an isolated area, the school had bars on the windows. That was a plus for the Terrorist Group. There were women in their group, and they were in charge of the women. They were rough looking characters.

Since they were held up in the school, there was plenty of food in the Cafeteria. The women and older girls had to do the cooking and cleaning up. The younger boys were responsible for taking the trash out, and the older youth were to keep the floor swept and mopped.

The women and girls were allowed to eat first, and the men and boys ate afterward. This was a frightening experience for the Villagers. None of them expected that someone would come to their Village and do this. The strangest thing was that the school was their meeting place if they had a disaster or something because they had extra food and water stored there.

Colonel Von Swog had all of the hostages brought to the meeting. He told them that their goal was to get what they came for and to get out of there quickly. He told them that they must get out before Soldiers are sent.

He said, "We will do whatever it takes to get what we want. Is that Clear?"

The Village people answered at the same time, "Yes, Sir."

Later Capt. Schmidt asked, "If some of the men try to attack us, what do we do, Sir?"

Colonel Von Swog answered and said,

"Let them know if they try anything, their love ones will be killed."

Enid Von Platt asked. "Are there any special instructions for us," (She was asking for the women in the Terrorist Group.)

Colonel Von Swog said, "We will meet Tomorrow morning at 2100 hour and I will divide everyone up, and you will get your instructions then."

What time do you want us to bring the Hostages out?" Asked Capt. Schmidt.

"Bring the women and girls at 1800 hour (6:00 a.m.), so they can prepare breakfast. Have the men here by 1900 hour (7:00 a.m.).

I will talk with them while they eat," said Colonel Von Swog. "Just remember to line them up as you bring them in to eat. I am sure that we won't have a problem with anyone trying to escape."

CHAPTER 4

SHATTERED DREAMS

Joe had received an honorable discharge from the Army with many medals and recommendations. He was one of the best Tactic Team Leaders that the Army had. Joe and Lydia were trying to put this experience behind them.

When the news came on that evening after Joe and Lydia had put the kids to bed, they couldn't believe their ears. They both felt an uneasiness in their hearts. Lydia's first thought was, "Who are they going to send to rescue these people?"

Joe said, "Those people must be crazy. Why would they want to hold innocent people hostage? Did you hear what they are asking?"

"Yes, I did. That is scary. That could be dangerous for everyone. What make people do things like that?" Lydia asked.

"In some countries, the boys are trained at an early age to be a Terrorist. Sometimes as young as eight years old. Therefore, they don't know any better because they were programmed early in life," Joe said.

Lydia asked, "What do you think is going to happen to those people in the Village?"

"It depends on a lot of things. The Army will need to send a Special Tactic Team to rescue them. That's what I used to do. The Army makes it a Secret Mission to make sure none of the information leaks out to the wrong people. It keeps the leader and his team safe," Joe said.

Do you mean by Spies or Traders?" Lydia asked.

"Yes, like Spies. You never know who is on someone's payroll. It's important to try and keep the Tactic Team as safe as possible. And that is to keep from jeopardizing the Mission also." Joe replied.

"Honey, I thank God, you don't have to do that anymore. I was so afraid when you were gone, not knowing whether you were alive or not," said Lydia.

"Well, God blessed all of us, to get back safely. It's all behind us now. We need to pray for those families," he said.

Joe and Lydia were always concerned about other Soldiers and their families. Joe knew what it was like to have to leave his wife and he had sympathy for them. It's hard splitting a family, especially if one has to go into a war zone.

Joe thought, "We take things for granted and don't know what each day holds for us."

He was very grateful that he was blessed to make it back home to his family.

In the meantime, Mr. President had called Joe's previous Commanding Officer, Colonel David McBride.

"Is this Colonel McBride?" Asked Mr. President.

"Yes, Mr. President, how may I help you?" Asked Colonel McBride.

"Well, we have a grave situation. There is a new Terrorist Group that has taken a Village hostage. It could be a crucial situation, and we need your help," said Mr. President.

"I am at your service, Sir. How may I help you?" Asked Colonel McBride.

Mr. President said, "We need a Tactic Team for this Mission with a Tactic Team Leader who has a steady record of success. We need a fearless and firm leader. One, his men will follow him to their graves if necessary," said Mr. President.

"I needed an answer yesterday," said Mr. President.

"Alright Sir, I'm on it," said Colonel McBride.

"You figure out who the best man is for this job and don't call me. Wait for me to call you. We have to be very careful because we are dealing with some crazy people," said Mr. President, "And this involves regular civilians."

"Will do," said Colonel McBride.

"Goodbye, Sir."

"Goodbye," said Mr. President.

While Mr. President was talking with Colonel McBride, the situation was getting worse with The Terrorist Group. Mr. President received a call on his private line. The Caller said that it was urgent to get a Tactic Team together. Things are getting out of hand with

The Terrorist Group. They don't have any idea how many Terrorists are in the group.

Meanwhile, Colonel McBride was already going through the files to determine what Tactic Team was best to handle this situation. He had to make a quick decision and figure out the number of men needed for the team.

Mr. President called Colonel McBride back. He said, "Colonel McBride, we don't have the time that we thought we had. The Terrorist Group don't want to wait too much longer. It's imperative that we get a team together as soon as possible."

"Sir, I only know of one man and his squad who may be right for this job," said Colonel McBride.

"Who is this man?" Asked Mr. President.

Colonel McBride responded, "Sgt. Joe Stevenson, Sir. He had the best track record of all the Tactic Teams. On his last two Missions, there were no casualties on either side."

"Well, what are you waiting on? Get a hold of him right away," said Mr. President.

"Sir, there is one problem," said Colonel McBride.

"What might that be?" Asked Mr. President.

"When I sent him on his last Mission, I told him that was the last one. Joe was honorably discharged from the Army four years ago," said Colonel McBride.

"If he is the best Leader of all the teams you have had, we need him. You need to call him. I am sure there is some incentive to make it worth his while," said Mr. President.

Colonel McBride said, "Sir, he is married with three children. When he went on his last Mission, he had been married for three months. His wife found out she was pregnant after he left. But he didn't find out until he came home."

"What does that have to do with this?" Asked Mr. President.

"If he had known about the baby it would have been hard for him to do his job," said Colonel McBride.

"If this man is a Soldier and you explain how crucial the situation is, I believe he will go," said Mr. President. "Let him know how many lives are at stake."

"Yes Sir, I will try contacting him. He bought a home in a different area," said Colonel McBride.

Colonel McBride looked in the telephone directory for Sgt. Joe Stevenson. "I will give you some time to get things lined up and then I will call you. If there is a problem, leave a message for me at my office. Just say, "Code Man," and hang up. I will know it's a problem," said Mr. President. "I will talk with you then."

"Goodbye Sir," said Colonel McBride.

Colonel McBride has a job on his hand. He first has to find out where Sgt. Joe Stevenson lives. Then he has to convince him to go on this Mission.

The Colonel knows how Joe feels about his family, so he knows what he is up against to ask him to come back. He started looking in the phone directory for Joe Stevenson's phone number. He found it just as he thought he would. He dialed the number very slowly wondering just how to approach Sgt. Joe Stevenson. Then he heard the phone ringing, and someone answered.

"Hello," Lydia said.

"I am looking for Joe Stevenson," said Colonel McBride.

"Who's calling please?" Asked Lydia.

"This is Colonel McBride, and it's urgent that I speak with Joe if this is his number," he said.

Lydia went pale as she handed the phone to Joe.

Joe said, "Honey, what's wrong?"

Lydia could not say a word. She just kept trying to give Joe the phone. He thought maybe one of his parents had died or something. Her facial expression made him very nervous. Finally, He took the phone.

"This is Joe Stevenson. Who is this, please?"

"Joe, this is Colonel McBride. How are you doing?" He said.

Joe and Colonel had a personal relationship. When they weren't around other soldiers, he called him by his name. He was an older man, and Joe always called him Colonel. They had not spoken in the last year.

"I am well Colonel. What is the occasion?" Asked Joe.

"Well, I'm sure you have been watching the News. There's a situation caused by The Terrorist Group in the middle east. Joe, they are worse than any we have seen. The President called me and said we need to get a

Special Tactic Team together as soon as possible," said Colonel McBride.

"But why are you calling me, Colonel?" Asked Joe.

"I must be honest with you. There is no one else who holds a record like you, Joe. The President said he wanted the very best Tactic Team Leader. I went through all my files, and no one comes close to your track record. The President will be calling me back soon," said Colonel McBride.

Joe said, "Colonel, did you forget that I have served my time and have an honorable discharge?"

"Son, I did not forget, but the President said that we need you. He is willing to give you a great incentive. We need your expertise and war skills," said Colonel McBride. "There are hundreds of lives at stake here. They are civilians."

Meanwhile, Lydia had sat down with her mouth partially opened with tears running down her cheeks.

"Joe, if you will come and be our Leader, I will get all the other top Leaders under you to form your team. It's urgent that we get on this right away. I will let you think about it and I will call you early in the morning. You must have an answer because Mr. President will be calling me around mid-morning," said Colonel McBride. "Son, I'm sorry and hate to ask this of you but there is no one else."

"Alright Colonel. I will expect your call in the morning," said Joe. "Good night, Colonel."

"Bye Joe," said Colonel McBride.

Joe slowly sat down, and tears started running down his face. Lydia came and sat by him, and they hugged each other. They didn't have to say a word. They knew what was at stake and they expected a lot from Joe.

As they were crying, their shattered world was crumbling around them. This time it's more dangerous. Joe was thinking about his children.

He said, "I just don't believe this is happening all over again. I don't want to leave my family."

Lydia had composed herself. She said, "Honey, we must pray because there is nothing else we can do."

Joe said, "I know, but I don't want to leave you and the children. I know we must think of all those families held and how they feel."

"God will give us the answer," said Lydia.

Joe said, "I know what I have to do and I pray that God will protect and keep you all safe."

Lydia said, "Honey, don't worry about us. We will be alright. Those families in that Village are the ones who are in danger."

CHAPTER 5

JOE'S FAREWELL

The next morning Joe and Lydia got up a little earlier than usual. Neither one of them slept very well. Joe woke the children up because he didn't know if he would have time to say goodbye to them before leaving. He wanted to explain to the children why he had to go away.

Joe told the children that he wants to talk to them after breakfast. He didn't want to spoil their appetite and felt that they might cry also. While they ate breakfast, Joe and Lydia didn't talk too much.

The children were talking about what they wanted to do later that day. Joe told them, we will see depending on our schedule.

Linda said, "What is schedule, daddy?"

Joe said, "It's when you make plans to do several things. Every day when Mommie get up, she has to get Joseph ready for school. Then she has to feed him and take him to school and later pick him up from school. Do you understand?"

She said, "A little bit but it's O.K."

They all laughed. After breakfast, Joe explained to their children why he was going away. They had all of their meetings in the family room.

Joe said, "I know you guys may not fully understand what I have to tell you. You all are young, but I don't want you to worry. O.K?"

Joseph and Linda said, "Yes Daddy, in unison as they often do."

Joe said, "Daddy is going away for a while. I don't know how long I will be gone, but I want you all to keep doing your chores and be good."

Joseph said, "Why are you going away, Daddy?"

Joe said, "Some bad people in another country are holding some people hostage. That means they will not let the people leave their Village and they have guns."

Joseph asked, "What is Village?"

Joe said, "It's like a city. It's where people live."

"Oh. O.K.," Joseph said.

Joe continued, "I have to go and help the people in the Village. While I'm away, I want you all to obey Mommie and do what she tells you."

They said, "O.K. Daddy and we will pray for you."

Joe hugged Joseph and Linda and kissed them. He was getting emotional. He told them that he loves them very much. Then the phone ranged. Lydia and Joe looked at each other. Joe told the children to do their chores in their rooms. He didn't want them to see tears in his eyes.

Joe took the phone. He sat on the couch, and Lydia sat beside him. They knew it was Colonel McBride. Joe held Lydia's hand as he answered the phone.

"Hello," he said.

Colonel McBride said, "Good morning. Do you have an answer for me?"

"When and what time do you want me to come to the base?" Joe asked.

Colonel McBride said, "Can I pick you up in two hours?"

Joe said, "I'll be ready Colonel."

When he got off the phone, Lydia was in their bedroom packing things he would need. He still carries a copy of her poem that she wrote for him years ago, titled, "I'll Wait." Joe went to Lydia and took her in his arms and kissed her.

After that he just held her. He said, "I know you all will be all right. I love you and the children so much. I can't describe the pain in my heart, but I know, God will have his Angels watching over you all. I don't have any idea of how long I will be gone. It pains me to know that I won't be able to talk with you or the children and we won't be able to write to each other, but I still have my poem, "I'll Wait" in my wallet and will always take it with me. Lydia, you are my rock, and I love you so much. I know God sent you to me. I will be able to call you for a few minutes before we ship out but I won't be able to tell you where I am going. Everything as usual on these Missions have to be secret. Colonel McBride will be picking me up in two hours. I want to say my goodbyes to the children and you in the house." He took her hand, smiled and said in a gently voice,

"Can I get to know you better?"

Lydia responded by falling into his arms while giving him a very passionate kiss. They made love, and both were thinking, this may be our last time together. They cried together and later prayed that God would bless him again to come back to his family.

Thirty minutes before Colonel McBride was due to arrive as they sat with the children. Joe hugged each one of them real tight and told them that he loves them. It was a sad day in their home. Joe was going off to who knows where and they didn't know if they would ever see him again.

Colonel McBride is always on time. Joe gave the children another kiss and left them in the family room. He went to say his final goodbye to Lydia, and the phone rang. It was Colonel McBride calling to let Joe know to be ready to leave in five minutes. He pulled Lydia to him and gave her a long hard passionate kiss.

She said, "Joe this is not good-bye. God will bring you back to us."

He was so overwhelmed that he just held her. She burst into tears. Good byes are hard.

Lydia said, "I am going to miss you. You will constantly be in my prayers. Joe, I love you so much that I can't express it in words.

Joe kissed her one last time and took his backpack and went outside. Just as he stepped out of the door, Colonel McBride was pulling up.

Joe got in the car and didn't look back. He was afraid if he looked back, he would not go. Meanwhile, Lydia was in the house crying and praying. She remembered when he was shipped out three months after they were married.

This time she will have the children to keep her company and keep her busy. She prayed that he would be safe and would not have to be gone too long. The children are four, three and one years old. She doesn't want them to forget him.

Later Joe called Lydia and told her not to get upset with what he was about to divulge to her. He wants her to know the incentive the President has authorized for them since Joe agreed to lead the Tactic Team.

Joe said, "The President has authorized that our mortgage is to be paid off and for you to receive a monthly check of $4,000 per month while I am gone. If by chance that I don't make it back, the monthly check will increase to $6,000 for the rest of your life. You will receive written information to keep for your records. This way you won't have to worry about finances. Lydia broke down crying. Joe told her that everything will be alright and that God is good.

Lydia said, "I know, but I don't like the idea that something could happen to you. I don't want to lose you."

Joe said, "Honey, we have to have the same faith that brought me home before. We still pray to the same God, and he knows best. Just trust him and remember that I love you more than life itself. I must get off the phone now. Kiss the kids for me."

"I will kiss them for you," said Lydia.

Joe said, "Honey I don't know what I am up against but God willing, I will be back. I love you beyond measure. Take care of yourself and our children."

"I love you too Joe and please don't take any unnecessary chances. I'll wait for you as long as it takes," said Lydia.

"Until later but never goodbye my love," said Joe.

She said, "Later to you, my darling."

Lydia had already retired when Scott was one year old. Now she doesn't have to worry about money while Joe is gone. She will be very concerned about Joe because after he leaves, she will not have contact with him again until his Mission is over.

Joe's biggest concern is how fast they will be able to solve the problem so he can come back to his family. It will be Joe's job to strategize the rescue. He will have the best group of men working with him.

They know his reputation and respect him very much. It will be an honor for them to serve under him. When he was in the Army, he had earned all kind of awards and commendations. As Joe and Colonel McBride traveled to the base, the Colonel was feeling Joe's pain.

He said, "Son, I can imagine how you feel, and I am very sorry, but you are the best that we have for this Mission. This group seems to be the most vicious that we have encountered, therefore, we need the best man to lead this team. It happens to be you."

Joe said, "Colonel there is no need for an apology. I am here to serve my country, and I know God will take care of my family. I hate leaving my kids. Above all, I have to consider the families who are being held hostage also. It will work itself out."

"War causes a lot of pain and heartache, but we have to do our part," said Colonel McBride, My heart aches for you, son. You have my prayers."

"Since all the other leaders should be there by the time we get there, I will start briefing this evening, so we can get a head start on things," said Joe.

CHAPTER 6

JOE MET WITH HIS MEN

Colonel McBride and Joe finally arrived at the Base. All the leaders were there waiting for them. As they entered the room, the Soldiers started clapping for Joe. That let him know that they liked and respected him.

Joe went around the room and shook every mans' hand while greeting them. After that, he asked that they sit down. Then he prayed.

Joe said, "We have a lot of work to do, and I want all of your opinions and suggestions. Does this sound good to you all?"

"Yes, Sir!" They responded.

"When any of you come up with an idea or suggestion, please raise your hand, and we will hear you out," said Sgt. Joe Stevenson.

He went to the map that Colonel McBride already had set up for them. The Village was isolated from the highway. It was in a rural area, and the next town was miles away. He pointed out that they would have to be very careful going in there.

They will have to find a way to get into the school-yard without being seen. All the men knew that Sgt. Joe Stevenson was a Christian and had always tried not to kill anyone during a Mission. He had managed to bring all of his men back home from his missions. This group wasn't too afraid, even though this was going to be Sgt. Joe Stevenson's most dangerous Mission.

They felt confident because the leaders were tops in their group. Each man had training for Tactic Team Missions, and they were the best.

Sgt. Joe Stevenson said, "This is a two-step process. The first one, we have to work out, is how to get into the Village unseen. The second is how we will take them out without losing any of the hostages or our Team."

All ninety-nine Soldiers that have been summoned to help Joe are the same rank. Sgt. Joe Stevenson and his team scored the highest results of all the Tactic Team Missions. They all know that this can be a rough situation, but they are prepared to fight.

Sgt. Brandon Jones said to Sgt. Joe, Stevenson, "Sir, I think if we study the map, it may be best to go in at night. We can use our night vision lights."

"Instead of bullets, we can use sleep darts to put them to sleep. This way there won't be any sounds, and no one will be injured," said Sgt. Michael Tate.

"Ok," Sgt. Joe Stevenson said. "We will need to be divided into groups. It's 100 of us so we will be groups of ten. We will study the map and decide which area each group will be assigned."

Sgt. Marcus Bristle said, "Since we don't know how many there are, we can observe them in the early morning, a little before dawn."

"And how are we going to do that without them seeing us?" asked Sgt. Arthur Curry. "I guess we can use our night vision lights."

Sgt. Joe Stevenson said, "We can camouflage and hide in the trees. Then we can pinpoint their schedule and determine how many are there."

Colonel McBride said, "I can contact Sgt. Dustin Williams in supplies and find out about getting some sleep darts. From our report, the Authorities in the Village area thinks there may be about forty to fifty terrorists."

From the main road, Joe and his team would have to hike through woods in order not to be seen. The team would have to be very careful. The Terrorist leader Colonel Von Swog felt that they would be able to get what they want and get away with it.

Since they were in the backwoods, he felt that no one would know that they had the Village hostage until he made his demands. Meanwhile, Sgt. Joe Stevenson and his team are working on their plans to capture this group and rescue the Villagers. Since civilians are involved, they must be very careful with their plans.

Sgt. Dustin Williams called Colonel McBride back.

He said, "Sir, we have plenty of sleep darts. Just let me know how many you want, and I will have them ready for you."

"O.K., thank you," said Colonel McBride, "I will let you know the exact amount that we need."

Colonel McBride turned to Sgt. Joe Stevenson and said, "There are plenty of sleep darts in the supply room. About how many do you think you might need?"

Sgt. Joe Stevenson responded with, "About a thousand. Just want to make sure, not knowing if we will miss our targets at some point."

"It's good to have plenty, but with the night vision lights, we should be alright," said Sgt. Brandon Jones.

Sgt. Joe Stevenson had the Team to gather around so they could see the map of the Village. He started showing them the different areas that they can go in where there are a lot of trees. The best part about the trees, they are all close together like a forest.

He explained, "We will be up in the trees. This way the Terrorists won't know what hit them. We will make our move when they all are outside."

Sgt. Joe Stevenson had Sgt. Michael Tate to put the men in groups. They all, of course, wanted to be with Joe, but only nine could be with him. He put Sgt. Brand Jones, Sgt. Marcus Bristle, Sgt. Arthur Curry, and himself and five others with Sgt. Joe Stevenson.

"When we shoot the sleep darts, we all will hit at the same time. Each one of us will pick a target. We must quietly let each other know which target we are aiming at, so we don't hit the same one," said Sgt. Joe Stevenson. "Hopefully we will be able to execute our plan and be on target. Time is going to be a great factor as we do this. We will move swiftly as we attack."

Colonel McBride said, "Does everyone understand this mission?"

They all responded, "Yes, Sir!" Sgt. Joe Stevenson said, "We will strike the Terrorists who are on watch and work our way to the schoolhouse. We will surround them. Be careful that you don't shoot one of our men. Be ready because when we start moving, we will be moving fast, so they won't have a chance to react."

Sgt. Arthur Bristle asked, "Will we do a drill on this?"

Sgt. Joe Stevenson replied with, "Yes, early in the morning because we want to pull out the day after tomorrow. We will spend the day doing drills. You guys get a good night's sleep because we have our work cut out for us."

"How much time will we spend observing them," asked Sgt. Byron Hill.

Sgt. Joe Stevenson said, "We will spend two days and two nights watching them. That will help us execute our plan better. I think they all probably will be out early to drill. If there are no more questions, the meeting is over. I thank all of you for being a part of this team.

You all get some rest. We have work ahead of us. When we attack, we all must be alert and move as quietly and swiftly as possible. We don't want to give them time to think. They will be so surprised that they will be confused and this will be to our advantage."

"This plan is very unique because they will think that we are on the ground rather than up in the trees. It gives us a great advantage over them," said Sgt. Arthur Bristle.

"That's exactly what I want them to think," said Sgt. Joe Stevenson. "Confusing the enemy is the best tactic to use,"

CHAPTER 7

TEXTED MESSAGES

When the Village was first being taking over, a couple of adults managed to call the local Police Chief to let them know what was going on. They both had estimated that it was approximately forty to sixty Terrorists.

Mrs. Rhonda Davis and Mrs. Bridget Washington managed to hide their cell phones before the group was able to collect all the cell phones. They had turned them off so they wouldn't ring. At night when everyone was quiet, they would text messages to the Police Chief.

These ladies used one phone because they didn't want both phone batteries to be dead at the same time. They were keeping a tab on every new person that they saw, so they could determine how many Terrorists were there.

Mrs. Rhonda Davis texted that they would be careful and not text every night. She said they would only text when they have something new to report. Ten of the terrorists were women, and they were mean like as the men.

Since the school windows had bars on them, the Terrorists didn't have anyone in the room with them at night. They had all the men in one area and the women and children in a separate area. During the day, they let them all eat together, sometime.

The Police Chief was able to let them know that they were working on getting them out safely. During the meals, the ladies would pass the word to their husbands, and later they would share with the other men.

Mrs. Bridget Washington passed the word among the women to keep their children close to them. She and Mrs. Rhonda Davis let them know that help was on the way so they would be alert.

Mrs. Rhonda Davis told them, "The Soldiers are coming to rescue us. If you hear any shooting, fall to the floor. Be sure to tell your children, even if we are at a meal and tell them to stay close to you."

Mrs. Bridget Washington said, "We don't know when they will be here, but we do know they are working on a plan. Warn your children not to talk about this among themselves, so the terrorists don't hear them."

The Police Chief told Mrs. Rhonda Davis to make sure she and Mrs. Bridget Washington turn their cell phones off once he responds to their text.

Well, Sgt. Joe Stevenson and his Tactic Team arrived at Base Zero. That was what they named the area where they went. They arrived early on a Thursday morning. Joe had calculated if all went well, they should be able to pinpoint the Terrorists and captured all of them within a few days. He prayed with his men on arrival. The men put their gear and supplies in place and parked their vehicles in the storage shed in back.

Of course, the weather conditions will be a great factor in how well they will be able to execute their plan. Since the weather was clear, it meant they will be able to function better at night. They will have to be very careful during the day.

Right now, they will be about a mile from the site where the Villagers are hostages. Sgt. Joe Stevenson contacted the Police Chief before they arrived. He requested that the Police Chief have an up to date copy of the map of the school and surrounding area. He knew this was going to be a very delicate situation because there would be women and children involved. That will be the first mission he's gone on where citizens were Captives.

Sgt. Joe Stevenson knows everything has to be precise because, with children, it's more dangerous. When they start attacking, he wants to make sure the children will not be able to get in their way. If it's Gods' will, he wants to rescue the Villagers with no deaths.

He and his men will spend the day, getting all of their equipment and sleep darts together along with their water and snack supply. He plans to set up with each squad as if they are going to attack. They will be in the trees at night to observe the school ground and to make a note of the actions of the Terrorists. They will note what they do and what time.

Each squad will make the notation of what goes on in the area they are watching. The Tactic Team will note how many times some of the Terrorists go in and out of the schoolhouse. The Police Chief let Sgt. Joe Stevenson know what Mrs. Rhonda Davis and Mrs. Bridget Washington have been texting him about the Terrorists.

This information is a big help to him, so he will know how to plan his attack. Each squad will get instructions on what to do and when. They must be precise in their notes, especially to know exactly how many terrorists they see.

Sgt. Joe Stevenson and his team will be in trees for about two hours before daybreak. He wants to see their morning routine. Mrs. Rhonda Davis had texted the Police Chief that all the Terrorists come in when they are ready to eat. Everyone eats at the same time, except twenty guards.

This information was helpful to know because after they finished eating, it would be easy to count them as they come out. Colonel Von Swog didn't feel any great fear right away. He felt it would take longer for them to get Soldiers in the area. He didn't know that the Police Chief received a text the first day the Terrorists took over the Village.

This Terrorist Group was demanding a 747 jet and fifty million dollars. The President was more concerned that if they got what they wanted, they would not leave the Villagers alive. That is why Sgt. Joe Stevenson and his team had to be very careful in their plan of attack. He talked to his Team to explain how he felt they should do things. He told his team what his plan was and asked if anyone had questions.

Sgt. Arthur Curry asked, "Sir, how long do you think it will take before we can attack?

His response was, "We will watch them for two days and nights. It's imperative that we get their schedule down as soon as possible, then I will know when we will attack. We need to get these people out safely and as quick as we can. There was a question from Sgt. Michael Tate.

He said, "Sir once we get the number of the Terrorists, then each squad will know how many men or women that they need to take out."

"Once we observe their routine, we will know their locations, and it will be easier to perfect our plan," was Sgt. Joe Stevenson response. "Then we will pray and ask for directions on executing our plan. Tonight, we will start our observations. Men gather around so you all can see the map. We will take our sleep darts just in case someone sees us. "I have numbered the areas from one to ten."

Sgt. Brandon Jones said, "That means ten men to each squad and one squad to each area. That's great!"

"Well, I have chosen the leaders: Sgt. Brandon Jones #1, Sgt. Arthur Curry #2, Sgt. Michael Tate #3, Sgt. Marcus Bristle #4, Sgt. Byron Hill #5, Sgt. Neal Willis #6,

Sgt. Eric Cannon #7, Sgt. Aaron Smith #8, Sgt. Carlos Jimenez #9 and I am number #10. I am going to have the rest of the men pick a number from this bag. The number they pull will be the same as their leader's. Then whoever is left, will be with me," said Sgt. Joe Stevenson.

"Ahhhh!!" Said Sgt. Henry Winslow.

Sgt. Joe Stevenson said, "I want to be fair. This way no one will feel slighted. I know a lot of you guys wanted to be in my squad. I appreciate that, but all of your leaders are good men to work with."

"Yes Sir," they responded.

Sgt. Joe Stevenson said, "I numbered the areas so each squad will be in the area of his number. Does everyone understand? Get with your Leaders so you will know which area you will be in."

"Yes Sir," they all responded.

Sgt. Joe Stevenson contacted the Police Chief and told him to text and let Mrs. Rhonda Davis or Mrs. Bridget Williams know when they see a light flash like a light blew out. They plan to make their attack in three days. The attack will be at 8:00 p.m. but they have to observe the Terrorists for two days to get their schedule. If they need to change the time, he will let the Police Chief know so he can text them.

He wants them to stay together as much as possible and if they hear any shots to hit the floor. He is hoping that they will be able to pull this off without any gun-fire. But he just doesn't know if that will happen.

In the meantime, Colonel Von Swog has told his group that they will have a meeting in the morning, He wants to set his plan in effect. He wants to make sure his crew knows what to do when they get attacked. Of course, he is looking for the Soldiers to attack with bullets. Boy! They are going to be in for a surprise. He is planning to take some hostages to the plane once they get word that it is ready.

Colonel Von Swog made demands via the news station of what he wants. He warns that if anyone tries to stop them, they will kill all the Villagers. He said if they get what they came for, he will let the people go. But the President doesn't want to take any chances because when you get a group like this, they always lie.

The President had told Colonel McBride that he wants Sgt. Joe Stevenson's Tactic Team to try and get all the Villagers out if possible unharmed and whatever he needs, give it to him.

There is only one road leading to the school, so Colonel Von Swog feels that they will get what they want and get out of there. He warns that he does not want to see any Police or Soldiers. He had a meeting with the Villagers earlier and told them if they obey, no one would be hurt or killed. They only want what they came for, and they plan to leave.

Colonel Von Swog had given his men orders not to touch the women or girls. He told them that they were there for business only and not pleasure. He said if any one of them got out of order, he would kill them because he does not want extra problems on his hands.

Colonel Von Swog has given the President five more days to meet their demand. If he does not get what he wants, he will kill all the Villagers, starting with the children. He said his men must be permitted to leave when they are ready.

He plans to leave in five days at 8:00 a.m. and will send someone ahead to make sure the money is on the plane. The main airport is two hours from the Village, but they are planning to take a smaller plane to the big airport. His first concern is when they transition from that plane to the larger plane.

The President's Advisors had been trying to negotiate with Colonel Von Swog so he would agree to leave all the Village people behind. But he fears that they may have a bomb on the plane to kill him and his group. He feels that if he takes some of the Village children with him, that they will be safe and will be able to get away.

Sgt. Joe Stevenson's intends to stop the Terrorist Group from taking any of the Hostages. Also, he wants to try and capture all the Terrorists alive. He is a Christian and has always found a way to rescue hostages without killing anyone. His tactics are so unusual, and that's why all the men wanted to be with him. His teams have not suffered any serious injuries or death.

They know that Sgt. Joe Stevenson is a praying Soldier. He prays before embarking on all of his missions. Sgt, Joe Stevenson not only prays for his men but the enemies also. He knows most of those people have families and want to get home safely too.

The light of Christ just shines in Sgt. Joe Stevenson. When people meet him, they feel at ease and as if they have known him for a long time. He's what you call a down to earth person, and he is a friend for life. Sgt. Joe Stevenson is very family oriented. He grew up as an only child and has always wanted a family. Meanwhile, he called the Police Chief to ask him questions about the design of the school inside and how many entrances.

The Police Chief said, "I can do better than that. I can get you a copy of the blueprint of the school."

"That will be great," Sgt. Joe Stevenson said. "When I study the blueprints, I can let you know how to direct the Villagers when we get ready to go in. This way, none of them will be in danger if the Terrorists start shooting."

The Police Chief said, "I will wait for your call, and we will have Ambulances and Paramedics on standby in case someone gets hurt."

Sgt. Joe Stevenson said, "That will be great, Sir and I appreciate your cooperation. My team is trained to try not to have any casualties when we rescue Hostages. We plan to do everything in our power to get them out safely."

"I appreciate you all coming, and I am sure the Villagers do too. When you let me know when you plan to make your move, we will be ready on this end," The Police Chief said.

Sgt. Joe Stevenson said, "All right sir, I will send a man to pick up the blueprints. Once we study the blueprints, then I will be able to tell you when we will strike."

The Police Chief said, "We are not letting the News Media know everything that's going on. We just tell them we are trying to work out a solution."

"Thank you, sir. The less they know, the better because the Terrorists, I am sure are watching to see what our plans are," said Sgt. Joe Stevenson.

The Police Chief said, "I will wait for your call. Good-bye, son."

Sgt. Joe Stevenson said, "Good-bye Sir."

Sgt. Joe Stevenson got off the phone with the Police Chief. Now he will get the team together. When they get the blueprints of the school, they will be able to tell where the Villagers are in the school.

It's evening so Sgt. Joe Stevenson told the men that they have a busy day ahead of them tomorrow.

"I want you men to turn in early tonight because tomorrow we will work out the strategy of our attack," said Sgt. Joe Stevenson. "Sgt. Marcus Bristle and Sgt. Brandon Jones, I will be sending you all into town to pick up the blueprints. I will call the Police Chief to let him know that you are coming and are in civilian clothes."

"Yes sir, I will be ready early," said Sgt. Marcus Bristle.

"Sir, so will I," said Sgt. Brandon Jones.

Sgt. Joe Stevenson said, "The Police Station is in the next town, which is twenty minutes away from here, so be careful. I don't believe you will run into any trouble. I want you all to be very careful and watch your backs."

Sgt. Brandon Jones said, "Sir, we will be careful and will hurry back."

Sgt. Joe Stevenson went to his cot and sat down with Lydia and the children on his mind. He took out his poem that Lydia had written him years ago when he went on a mission. It was a charm for him to know his love would be waiting for him. He always carried this poem in his wallet and always read it periodically.

He loved Lydia more than life itself and felt closer to her each time he read her poem. He thought this is the kind of love that I always wanted. I thank you, Lord, for giving it to me. He took out his poem and began to read it:

I'll Wait (Lydia Poem)

I'll wait for you today and tomorrow, through all the heartache and sorrow. There will be trials and tribulations to strengthen our marital relations. God is controlling these events and knows where you will be. He will keep you safe in His arms and protect you from life's harms. When I awake, I pray that you are safe and that God will return you to our place. I'll wait no matter how long it takes, and when you return, its' sweet love we will make.

It's very lonely without you here, and I miss you so much, my dear. You have met a lot of people in life, but you chose me to be your wife.

I'll wait for you, days, months and years and on your return, there will be no more tears. I will wait until the day you come home, and it will be as if you were never gone.

After he read his poem, he prayed and then laid down and went to sleep with Lydia and the children on his mind.

CHAPTER 8

ATTACK PREPARATION

The next morning, Sgt. Marcus Bristle and Sgt. Brandon Jones your cooperation. headed out to town. In the meantime, Sgt. Joe Stevenson called the Police Chief. He let him know that they are on their way to pick up the blueprints of the school and are in civilian clothes.

Sgt. Joe Stevenson has the rest of the men getting their gear together for the attack. He wants to make sure they have everything in order. Each man will have a backpack with water, snacks, sleep darts, guns, and bullets. They will have guns in case they have a problem taking the Terrorists down with the sleep darts.

He does not want to jeopardize his men or the Villagers. In all the years, that he was a Tactic Team Leader, he was always prepared for the unexpected. When he made his plans, he made them well. The men on his team trusted him because he would come up with ideas of doing things, different from anyone else.

Sgt. Joe Stevenson has the best record in the history of the Army because he and his men survived every Mission they did. He is a Christian and never wanted to kill anyone. He always prayed and asked God to lead and direct him each time he was going on a Mission.

About an hour later, Sgt. Brandon Jones and Sgt. Marcus Bristle returned with the blueprints of the school.

Sgt. Joe Stevenson asked, "Did you all have any problems?"

Sgt. Brandon Jones said, "No Sir.

Everything went well. The Police Chief said that the Terrorists only went to the school and wasn't seen anywhere else."

"It makes sense that they would go where there were a lot of people. If they ran into trouble, they would have hostages," said Sgt. Joe Stevenson. "I need to meet with all the leaders in an hour because we need to go over a few things for the drill."

Sgt. Joe Stevenson and the other nine leaders went into the room where they held their meetings. He had to inform the other leaders the way he wanted the attack to go. He explained by dividing the team into ten groups; they could cover more ground without being seen. They already had their number to the areas they would cover.

In the meeting, Sgt. Joe Stevenson said, "Each of us needs to instruct our group how to branch out and surround the school. We need to be up in the trees and need to be shooting the sleep darts fast. We don't want the Terrorist group to figure out where we are."

Sgt. Bryon Hill said, "We need to show the men in our group on the map, the areas they need to cover."

"Yes, that will work, so we don't end up shooting each other, "said Sgt. Eric Cannon."

"We want to make sure we are on one accord. When we attack, and the Terrorists start falling, they won't know what hit them. If anyone of them manages to fire his gun, they will be shooting low in the trees," said Sgt. Joe Stevenson.

"We have to make sure all the men take their communication earphones. They will be able to talk to each other," said Sgt. Aaron Smith.

Sgt. Carlos Jimenez said, "When we drill tomorrow, we can check our earphones to make sure they have batteries and are working well."

Sgt. Joe Stevenson said, "The main thing, we must prevent the Terrorists from getting into the school. We don't want them to get to the Villagers."

"We need to make sure that none of them go back into the gym also. Once the Terrorists are outside, we want to make sure that we get all of them. Each man will have twenty sleep darts, but we are taking guns also, in case we have a problem," said Sgt. Joe Stevenson.

The next morning, they did their drills, and it went very well. All the men were anxious to get this over with, so they could go home. The sooner it's over, the faster they can go home. They have made their plans, and they are ready to go and observe the Terrorists.

The Police Chief called Sgt. Joe Stevenson and said, "A group of Soldiers will be standing by with trucks to carry the Terrorists in after they are asleep. The sleep darts will keep them out for about three hours, and that would be plenty of time to haul them off to the FBI."

"We appreciate that Sir. When we get them down, we will put their bodies in one place, so the Soldiers can quickly take them out," said Sgt. Joe Stevenson.

The Police Chief also said, "We will have buses ready to bring the Villagers out of there. We are praying for them and hope all goes well."

"We will start observing the Terrorists tonight,' said Sgt. Joe Stevenson.

If we can get their set schedule, then we will come tomorrow morning and check on them again. The next day if the schedule is the same, we will send our signal the third night to the Villagers at 8:00 p.m." said Sgt. Joe Stevenson.

"I will let the women know and remind them to keep their children close. They will let their husbands know also," said The Police Chief. "I think that covers everything. We thank you, men, for coming to help us. I will talk to you later."

Sgt. Joe Stevenson said, "Ok Sir and we appreciate your cooperation. Good-bye."

Sgt. Brandon Jones said, "Men, let's get busy and start preparing for tonight. Make sure that you carry your earphones and that they have good batteries in them."

Sgt. Joe Stevenson went to the map where he had circled each Leaders area. The men gathered around him so he could direct them. He warned that they had to be quiet.

Sgt. Joe Stevenson said, "We will go in when it gets dark, and we will pull out about 18:00 hour (6:00 a.m.)."

After they had their instructions, Sgt. Joe Stevenson dismissed them. He was thinking about Lydia and the children, wishing he could talk to them. They all missed their families as well. His number one concern was to get them home safely.

The President had said this is the largest number of people that have been hostage. He hopes that Sgt. Joe Stevenson and his Team will be able to capture these Terrorists and save all the hostages. They don't know if more Terrorists in their group may come later. Right now, they are working on a wing and a prayer.

Sgt. Joe Stevenson is praying that they will be able to end this situation day after tomorrow. If they can do that, they can be home in about a week. After they come back from a Mission, they have a briefing at Headquarters. Each man has to report on their position and how and what they did to execute their mission.

When they were ready to leave, Sgt. Joe Stevenson said, "Men gather around and get on your knees. We must give honor to God and pray before we go to battle. God said, "The battle is His. We must have faith that God is in control."

After he finished praying, he asked if anyone had any questions about the Mission or the areas. Now they are all ready and about to head out to the school. They are going to drive about a half mile but are going to walk the rest of the way. Where they are staying is about a mile from the school.

Sgt. Joe Stevenson said, "When we get to our areas, climb in the highest and thickest trees. When we attack, we will all shoot sleep darts at the same time. They will probably think we are shooting guns with silencers. If any of them get to shoot his gun, he will be shooting low in the woods, thinking we are on the ground.

As they trudged through the woods,

Sgt. Michael Tate said, "This is the lightest load we have ever had on a Mission. (He chuckled)."

"Well, just pray that we will have success with these sleep darts," Sgt. Eric Cannon said.

"Alright, we are getting close. Be quiet and keep your eyes open," said Sgt. Carlos Jimenez.

"Be sure to write everything in detail that you see them do," said Sgt. Joe Stevenson.

As they were approaching the school, they split up. Sgt. Joe Stevenson had mapped out their areas so they would surround the school. Each group went to their designated areas. When they got to their areas, they climbed trees where they would be able to see the school ground.

The playground was between the Gym and the schoolhouse. This where the Terrorists gathered in the mornings and evenings. After the groups got situated in trees, they could see that they had two guards on each corner of the schoolhouse in the back and two on each corner in the front. The Gym had three doors, one in the front, the back and the side. There were two guards at each door of the Gym.

They also had six guards walking the yard and four guards at the road entrance to the school. Sgt. Joe Stevenson and his team stayed in the trees until 2200 hour (10:00 p.m.) that night. He passed the word for them to start descending from the trees so they could leave. He warned the men to be very careful as they were getting out of the trees. They all met up about a quarter of a mile from the schoolhouse. When they all reached their meeting place, then they headed out.

On the way, back to where they were staying, Sgt. Joe Stevenson said, "When we get back, we will compare our notes. Then we will start putting our final plan together. After we go back in the morning, we will see if there is a change. If there is no change, we will attack tomorrow night."

Sgt. Dustin Williams asked, "Are we going to leave at 14:00 (2:00 a.m.) in the morning?

Sgt. Joe Stevenson said, "Yes, we will pull out at that time. I want you all to get some rest because we will have a briefing after we get back this morning. Be prepared for the attack day after tomorrow at 2000 hour (8:00 p.m.) I think we should observe one more day."

"We will be ready Sir, said Sgt. Neil Willis. "Let's get it over and go home."

The men knew that they had to be precise with their sleep darts. They were a little anxious because they had never used sleep darts before. But they trusted Sgt. Joe Stevenson. He had the best track record of all the Tactic Team Leaders. Everyone had great respect for him also.

Sgt. Aaron Smith will send the signal when it's time. It's important that the Police Chief know what time they are going to flicker the light. Mrs. Rhonda Davis and Mrs. Bridget Williams will watch for the light, and they will know it's time for the attack. Then they will have everyone spread their covers on the floor and lay down.

Sgt. Joe Stevenson called the Police Chief. He told him to asked the ladies if they could find any thick string or belts or electrical cords that they could tie the doors. On school doors, usually you have to push down to open them, and they are where you can tie them together. If they are tied together, no one will be able to come inside. He wants to make sure none of the Terrorists will be able to get in the schoolhouse when they attack.

As soon as they see the light flicker, Sgt. Joe Stevenson, wants Mr. Davis and Mr. Williams to get to the doors and tie them together. He wants to make sure no one sees them from the outside. They said that they would be careful and everyone will lay down.

Mrs. Rhonda Davis and Mrs. Bridget Williams will put the things to tie the doors where their husbands will be able to get to them. The men will be doing the same things the women will be doing. When they see the light flicker, they will all lay low too.

They are anxious and a little nervous waiting for the attack. That will be an experience the Villagers will never forget. The Villagers never dreamed that they would ever be in this kind of danger. In their Village, the people are like a big family. Most of them are related. Now it's time for The Tactic Team to leave to do their final observation of the Terrorists. Sgt. Neal Willis told the men that it is time to get their gear ready to head out.

Sgt. Neal Willis said, "We will be leaving in thirty minutes. Sgt. Joe Stevenson, do you have last minute instructions for the men, before we leave?

Sgt. Joe Stevenson said, "Men make sure you have your firearms with you also. We want to be ready for the unexpected."

The men responded with, "Yes, sir!"

When they got back to their areas around the school, they climbed into trees. They are about a half block from the school. Their night vision lights let them see the Terrorists with no problems. As the men watched the Terrorists, they did everything the same as before.

That was a relief because it would be easy to finalize the plan of attack. They timed how the guards around the school and Gym changed shifts. Now Sgt. Joe Stevenson thinks that tomorrow evening, they can give their signal that the attack will be at 8:00 p.m. As the night went by, nothing different happened.

All the men were noticing that the routine was the same as before. This was pleasing to them because of Sgt. Joe Stevenson. He would not have to change his plan of attack. They knew with no changes that they would be able to execute their Mission and get out of there quickly. Most importantly, they were all praying that no one would be hurt or killed. Even though they were going in with sleep darts, they still were a little nervous. They had never used this method before but being with Sgt. Joe Stevenson, they believed in prayer. They began to see a lot of things that God worked out for them. Some of the Soldiers were already believers but a few had doubts that were soon taken away.

All the men were happy to be in the company of Sgt. Joe Stevenson. He has a good personality and he was very smart. His career record was widely known also. There was no one who didn't like him. He was firm but a very compassionate person. He had a reputation of bringing his men back from his missions.

Everyone knew that any time they went on a mission, it was possible that they all may not make it back safely. So far, Sgt. Joe Stevenson had been able to bring his Soldiers back alive and unharmed. He knew that this was through prayer and trusting God.

CHAPTER 9

THE ATTACK

The next morning Sgt. Joe Stevenson told the Police Chief to text the ladies and let them when they see the signal, to get on the floor and start praying.

The Police Chief said he would let them know. Once Mrs. Rhonda Davis and Mrs. Bridget Williams get the word, they will let their husbands know when they go to breakfast.

So, tonight when they see the flash, they all will start praying. You see, prayer is powerful in numbers. And God hears all our prayers. As the day goes by, everyone is a little anxious. The Tactic Team, as well as the Villagers, will be glad when this is over, and they can get back to normal. Although for the Villagers, it will never be the same but something they will never forget.

Meanwhile, the Tactic Team have made sure that they have everything ready for tonight. So now they all will be going to sleep so they will be rested and prepared. Soldiers on Tactic Teams are trained to be able to stay awake for several days with no sleep.

That comes from a grueling training that they must go through to learn to do this. Little food is required as long as water is available. Usually, there are plenty of protein bars. Most of the team won't sleep because of the anxiety, but they will rest.

They will be up by 5:00 p.m. and Sgt. Aaron Smith will give the signal at 8:00 p.m. They will gather just in case Sgt. Joe Stevenson has last minute instructions. And they always pray before heading for an attack. They all are praying that this attack will be successful so they can go home to their families in a few days.

As the day is coming to a close, the Villagers are giving their children last minutes instructions. They are planning to keep their children close to them.

Mrs. Rhonda Davis said, "It won't be long before we see the light flash. When we see the light flash we all will lay down and start praying."

"If you hear any gunshots, don't be afraid and don't make any noise," said Mrs. Bridget Williams. "Everything is going to be alright. By this time tomorrow, we should be in our homes."

Meanwhile, Mr. Davis and Mr. Williams are waiting to see the flash so they can crawl to the doors and bind them with belts and a piece of rope that was in a closet. Sgt. Joe Stevenson figured this was the best way to keep the Villagers safe. Since the Terrorist Group will be on the outside, none of them will be able to get into the school. He plans to try and keep all the Villagers as safe as possible.

Colonel Von Swog and his group think they are going to be able to get their demands on tomorrow and leave. He plans to take some of the women and children to guarantee their escape. But what he doesn't know is that Sgt. Joe Stevenson doesn't plan for them to leave at all.

Sgt. Joe Stevenson is a Christian and always pray and ask God for guidance when he's on a Mission. He learned at an early age that you have to have faith and believe that God will never let you down. On his last Mission, four years ago, his team rescued a group of Soldiers. They were able to rescue them with no lives lost on either side.

That made Sgt. Joe Stevenson and his team have the best record of all the Tactic Teams. That was why the President of the United States wanted him to lead this team. Since this was the first time they had to rescue Civilians, he wants to try and save all of them, especially since children and women are involved.

Well, it's time for them to pull out. Sgt. Aaron Smith will give the signal as he gets close. When he gives the signal, the team will already be in place. Then he will join his group.

Before they leave, Sgt. Joe Stevenson said, "Men, I want to thank you all again for joining me on this Mission. Let's pray."

They all got on their knees as Sgt. Joe Stevenson starts praying, "Dear Heavenly Father, our Lord and Savior, we thank you for blessing us to be here. We ask that you guide and direct us on this Mission. Lord, if it's your will, please let us rescue the Villagers with no loss of life. We thank you for blessing and keeping our families while we are away. Lord, we ask forgiveness of our sins of omission and commission. We pray that you will keep us on the straight and narrow road. Please cover us in your Son Jesus' blood as we attack tonight. We thank you, Lord, in advance and pray for our enemies and their families as well. We give you all the honor, all the glory and all the praise in your Son Jesus' name. Amen, Amen, Amen," as Sgt. Joe Stevenson finished praying. They all said, "Amen."

Now they are headed to the school. When they attack, they will be in the trees. The Terrorists will think they are on the ground among the trees. As they neared the school, Sgt. Aaron Smith gave the light flash signal. When the Villagers saw the light flash, they all got on the floor and started praying.

Just as Sgt. Aaron Smith got to his group, the Tactic Team attacked. They were communicating with each other through their headsets. The Terrorists could not hear them. The Terrorists started falling before they realized what was happening.

Colonel Von Swog had just gone over to talk with one of the guards at one corner of the school. When the guard fell, Colonel Von Swog immediately laid by him. The Tactic Team was shooting sleep darts. Colonel Von Swog stayed there as if he was dead. He wasn't sure exactly what was happening.

They were hit with full force and so fast, the Terrorists didn't have a chance to think. One of the Terrorist got off several rounds with his automatic gun, but he didn't hit anyone because he was shooting into the woods below the trees. The local Soldiers were close by waiting for it to be over so they could come in and get the Terrorists while they were still sleeping from the darts.

The local Soldiers were about a block away with trucks to haul off the Terrorists. Sgt. Joe Stevenson and his team were so swift that they had all the Terrorists down within minutes. Then the signal was given for the local Soldiers to come in to pick up the Terrorists. They would sleep for about three hours.

As the local Soldiers picked up all the Terrorists, they were doing a head count. Sgt Green, the local Soldier, said, "One Terrorist is missing."

Sgt. Joe Stevenson instructed his men to do an intensive search around the whole area. They could not find the missing person. He had them to check the Terrorist ranks on their sleeves. They realized that they had all of them except, Colonel Von Swog.

Sgt. Henry Winslow started stationing men around the school and Sgt. Joe Stevenson had his men around the gym and even had them to check the inside of the gym. Colonel Von Swog had vanished. The local Soldiers finished loading the Terrorists in the trucks,

The Terrorists was going to be locked up at an FBI facility. After the local Soldiers had taken the Terrorists away, they would be interrogated by the FBI Agents. Sgt. Joe Stevenson and his Team double checked the areas. That included shining lights in the trees. Then he got on the horn to let the Villagers know it was safe to unlock the front doors of the school.

Once they got into the school, Sgt. Carlos Jiminez asked if everyone was alright. And told them buses would be there shortly to take them home. He also let them know that the FBI would later question all of them about the Terrorist Group.

The Villagers were shouting and thanking God and the Tactic Team from saving them. They were very grateful for the Tactic Team. They were hugging everyone, including Sgt. Joe Stevenson and his men. Some were crying with happiness. And they started hugging their husbands and sons. Finally, the buses arrived to take the Villagers home.

That was one of the best days for them because they were not sure if they were going to make it out alive. After the buses left with the Villagers, Sgt. Joe Stevenson and his men stayed behind and doubled checked the areas around the school in the daylight. They did not find Colonel Von Swog.

Joe's Most Dangerous Mission

They would be there for at least one more day to do their reports; then they would be headed home. They were all excited about this. But before they left the school ground, Sgt. Joe Stevenson and his men gathered and prayed before leaving. They thanked God, for safety and getting the Villagers out alive.

Also, they prayed that Colonel Von Swog would not be able to regroup and Terrorize any more people. Then they went back to where they were staying to do their reports. The Police Chief called Sgt. Joe Stevenson and told him that they wanted to celebrate with them on tomorrow.

He said the Villagers wanted to honor and thank them for their rescue. He accepted but told the Police Chief that they had to be heading for home by 4:00 p.m. After he got off the phone with the Police Chief, he told the men about the 12:00-noon celebration for the next day. He reminded them to have all their gear ready, so after the celebration, they would be heading home.

That was good news, and they were thankful that this rescue went well. In fact, this was the easiest Mission they had ever executed. Sgt. Joe Stevenson reminded the men that it was totally by God's grace.

Sgt. Henry Winslow said, "We will have good food tomorrow!"

The rest of the men joined in with, "Yeah!

Each man had to write a report on their experience here. So, they all got busy. After they finished their reports, they went to bed. They were all thinking about the food that they would be eating on tomorrow. Real cooking sounded good to all of them.

But the best joy, was no one was hurt or killed. The Tactic Team would be headed home immediately after the celebration. The Villagers wanted to show their appreciation and to thank them again. The Tactic Team was looking forward to some good food. They had not eaten regularly because of the Mission.

They were trained to go without regular food for days and live on protein bars, water, and gatorade. Home cooking was appealing to all of them. And they were anxious to get back to their families also.

CHAPTER 10

JOE'S AWAKENING

Finally, Lydia told the children that it was time for them to leave. They planned to go to the movies after they left the park. The children were having such a good time. They were never anxious to leave the park because they loved it.

Joseph said, "Mommie, do we have to go now?"

Lydia said, "It will be dark in an hour, and our movie starts then. Don't you want to see it from the beginning?"

Joseph said, "Yes, Mommie."

Lydia said, "I guess we had better wake Daddy up. He must have been tired. I am surprised that he hadn't woke up."

She and the children went to Joes' favorite spot, where he was sleeping. When they got there, he was still asleep.

Lydia said, "Honey, as she gently nudged Joe.

It's time to wake up if we are still going to the movies."

Joe woke up with a startled look in his eyes as he looked around.

Lydia said, "Are you alright!"

He said, "Have I slept for a long time? Wait a minute! We just captured the Terrorists."

She said, "Honey, what are you all right? We brought the children to the park, and you were tired, so you took a nap."

Joe said, "Oh my goodness, I must have been dreaming. I have been thinking about the Village people who are being held hostage by that Terrorist Group."

Lydia said, "We promised to take the children to the movies when we leave here. Do you think it would be best to postpone it until another time?"

"You know I hate to break a promise to the children, but I think I need to postpone this. I want to talk with Colonel McBride," said Joe.

"Colonel McBride? What do you need to discuss with him?" Asked Lydia.

"When I tell you about this dream I had, you will understand. I believe God gave me away for the Tactic Team to capture the Terrorists without possibly losing any lives," said Joe.

"Honey, are you planning to volunteer to help them rescue these people?" Asked Lydia.

Joe said, "No, baby. I just believe that I need to tell Colonel McBride about this dream and how we rescued the people in my dream. If I can see a map of the area and the surroundings, I might be able to help them without going anywhere."

Joe took Joseph and Linda in his arms and hugged them. He told them that he had a dream about how to help a lot of people.

He said, "We are going to postpone the movies for today. I need to talk with Colonel McBride. I hope you guys won't be upset, but I will make it up to you all. Daddy has some business he must take care of. O.K.?

Joseph and Linda said, "It's O.K. Daddy."

"I love you guys so much. Let's go home. I need to make that phone call," said Joe.

Lydia said, "O.K. let's pack up so we can go home. Make sure all the trash is in the cans."

The children sang out, "O.K., Mommie."

After they got packed up and headed for home, Joe and Lydia were in deep thought. Joe was overwhelmed with his dream. Lydia was afraid that Joe might miss going on the Missions and want to start back. Joes' thoughts were that his dream was God's way of showing him how the Attack could be carried out without anyone getting hurt or killed.

As soon as they arrived home, the children started getting their backpacks and got out of the car. Whenever they went someplace, Lydia always packed the children snacks. Joe called Colonel McBride as soon as they got everything out of the car and got the children settled. He helped Lydia bathe the children and put on their pajamas. Finally, he had time to call Colonel McBride.

Ring! Ring! Colonel McBride was at home. He answered his phone, "Hello."

"Hello Colonel McBride, this is Joe Stevenson. How are you?"

"I am fine. Is anything wrong? Is your family alright?" Said Colonel McBride.

"No Sir, they are fine. I had an omen or should I say a dream. I believe God has given us a way to free the Village people with as less harm as possible," Joe said.

"Let me hear about this. It sounds like it's interesting," said Colonel McBride.

"Well, I had this dream of using sleep darts on the enemy rather than real bullets. I would like to meet with you and give you the full details. I am sure you will find this very interesting," said Joe. "It was so real that when I woke up, I thought I was on the Mission."

Colonel McBride said, "Is Wednesday good for you, about noon? If you come to the base I will buy you lunch."

"Alright, I will see you then," said Joe.

When Joe got off the phone and he went into the bedroom to pray. He asked God to give him directions and clarification of his dream. He believes it was too clear for it not being from God. After Joe prayed, he went into the family room and watched movies with his family.

When he sat down by Lydia, she leaned over and kissed him lightly on the lips. She knew everything was going to be alright. While he was in the bedroom praying, she was in the bathroom praying. She asked

God to guide her husband and keep him safe and to continue to protect their children.

After they put the children to bed, Joe told Lydia about his dream. He let her know that he felt it came from God and that he wanted to share his dream with Colonel McBride.

Joe told Lydia that he believed this would be a new way to fight the enemy. There will be fewer deaths if it's a hostage situation.

Joe believed in God and prayer very strongly because, on all of his missions, they have never killed anyone. He believed that it was God's will for him not to have blood on his hands. He trusted God to bring him a loving wife, and now he has the family he had always wanted. He stayed a virgin until he married and the best part about, so did Lydia.

She had told him that she decided when she was a teenager that she would not have sex until she was married. Strangely enough, Joe made the same pledge as a teenager. Both had prayed that God would send them the right mate.

CHAPTER 11

JOE MET WITH COLONEL MCBRIDE

When Joe met with Colonel McBride, he was very anxious to tell him about his dream. He told the Colonel how the women had managed to text the Police Chief and informed him of the number of Terrorists that was there. He said in the dream everything went as planned.

Joe said, "Colonel, will you see if you can get a map of the area and blueprints of the school? I believe that I can be helpful to your Tactic Team, once I see the map and blueprints."

Colonel McBride said, "I will request them right away."

He buzzed his secretary so she could request those things for him. He told her to let them know that he needs them right away.

The map of the school area and the blueprints were faxed to the Colonel. When Joe saw them, they were as they were in his dream. He jumped up and said, "Oh my God! Colonel, they are the same as my dream!"

"Are you sure?" Asked Colonel McBride.

Joe said, "Yes Sir, with tears in his eyes. Colonel do you know what this means?"

Colonel McBride said, "I think I'm getting the picture."

Joe said, "I can instruct the Team on exactly how to execute their Mission."

Colonel Mc Bride asked Joe if he could stay a few hours because the Tactic Team Members would be meeting at 2:00 p.m.

"It's no problem, Sir. I can be here as long as you need me," Joe said.

Colonel McBride thanked Joe, and they went to eat. He said most of the men would be arriving a little early. The Colonel figured by the time he and Joe finished eating, it would be close to 2:00 p.m. He felt if all the men had arrived, they could go right into the meeting. This way, there would be plenty of time if the men had a lot of questions for Joe.

By now Joe is so wired up, he just couldn't believe it. He knows God works in ways that we will never understand, but that shook him. They went to the Base Cafeteria, and when they got there, they went to the bathroom to wash their hands.

Joe said, "I will be out in a little while Colonel. I want to pray."

Colonel McBride said, "Alright, I will get us a table. What do you want to order?"

Joe said, "A ham sandwich and salad will do. Thank you, Sir. Please order me a small piece of cake on the side."

He went into a stall and let the top of the toilet down and sat on it. He started praying, "Dearly heavenly

Father, I am coming to you as your humble servant. I thank you for blessing me to be able to lead men on these Missions. I am asking forgiveness of my sins and asking for your guidance. Lord, I don't want to steer this Tactic Team wrong. Please guide my speech and direct me as I tell them about my dream. Lord, please have mercy on them and let them know these directions are not mine but yours. Protect each one of them and bring them back safely. Lord, I thank you in advance for using me to show them how to do this. I thank you, in Jesus name. Amen."

After Joe and Colonel McBride had finished eating, they went back to the meeting room. All the Soldiers on Base were familiar with Joe's reputation as being the best Tactic Team Leader the Army had ever had. He had been discharged from the Army five years ago. These men did not know him personally but had heard of him. He was a legend.

Colonel McBride introduced Joe when they were ready to start the meeting. They all stood up clapping. Joe went around and shook each Soldier's hand, thanking them. It was eighty soldiers present. After they settled down, Joe began to tell them about his dream.

Then he told them that the map of the school area and the blueprints were as his dream. They were shocked.

One said, "Oooh, my goodness!"

Another one said, "Holy Cow."

And they started laughing. Joe explained that God had given him this revelation. They put the map of the school area up first. He explained how they observed the Terrorists from the trees. When he told them that they used sleep darts, it blew their minds. They had never heard of such.

Joe said, "I know most of you have heard the story of Gideon in the Bible."

They all said, "Yes, Sir!"

He said, "We never know how God is going to work out a situation. That's why we need to be in prayer and ask Him for guidance. Most of all, we have trust what He tells us."

Colonel McBride said, "Well does anyone have objections to doing it God's way?"

All the Soldiers said, "No Sir!"

"Well I want you all to listen very carefully to

"Well, I want you to listen very carefully to Sgt. Joe Stevenson. He will giv7e you explicit details of his revelation. You may want to take notes. That's why there are pads and pens in front of all of you. Your lives could depend on it," continued Colonel McBride.

Joe did everything with the Soldiers as he did with his men in his dream. He picked the leaders for each group and numbered them, 1-9. He had the Leaders, to write their names on ten small pieces of paper. Then they were all put in a bowl and shook up. Joe had numbered the map around the school in ten places. The Leader was the 10th Soldier in the group.

Those areas were marked 1-10. Joe had two drawings. One was so the Leaders could pick a number which would be the area. The second drawings were for the Soldiers to get a number to determine their Leader.

It would be ten Soldiers in each group, and their area would have the same number that they had. Joe was very organized in all of the things he did. After they all understood what their numbers meant, they grouped according to their number. Joe explained his dream to them in detail. He told them that it was important that they did everything he told them. The Soldiers were blown away by his dream. He agreed to work with them for a week and drill them before they left.

Colonel McBride was so thankful for Joe taking time to do this. He called the President and explained Joe's dream and told him that he was briefing the Team. The President said that Joe was to be rewarded beyond measure if he pulled this off.

Well, it was time for the Tactic Team to leave for their Mission. Joe was there to pray with them and see them off. After the Tactic Team got to their destination, they couldn't believe that Joe had described the place exactly as it was. They now felt more confident about the situation.

The first couple of days, they did their drills and went and to observed the Terrorists from the trees, just as Joe had told them. The finality of it went like Joe had said. They rescued the Villagers with no deaths. Before they attacked, they pray like Joe said he did.

After everything was over, the Villagers gave them a celebration with plenty of well-cooked food. And they were happy to all be going home unharmed,

When the returned home, the President came to the Base and shook every Soldiers hand who was on that Team. Joe was there also. They made plans for a big celebration and awarded all the Soldiers including Joe.

The President had Joe's home mortgage paid off and allocated him $4,000 a month for the rest of his life. The President asked Joe if he would supervise the future Tactic Teams when needed. Of course, he agreed.

Joe was in awe and could not believe it. When he told Lydia, they were crying and praising God at the same time. The Leaders of the Tactic Team told Joe that he had made a believer out of them. And from now on, they will pray before they do any Mission. Joe was so overwhelmed that tears were rolling down his face.

On the way home from the Base, Joe talked to God and thanked Him all the way home. A week later, Joe and Lydia received the deed to their home, marked paid in full. Two weeks later, Joe received his first $4,000 check. They cried, they prayed, and they cried tears of joy!

Note** All you have to do is be obedient and trust God. But most of all, you have to put Him first in everything you do. Trust and He will bring you through. This story is fictional, but the part about God is true. You need to develop a personal relationship with Him, and you will find out for yourself, He is REAL!